Happily Ever Arthur

Maverick
Early Readers

'Happily Ever Arthur'
An original concept by Jenny Jinks
© Jenny Jinks 2023

Illustrated by Michelle Simpson

Published by MAVERICK ARTS PUBLISHING LTD
Studio 11, City Business Centre, 6 Brighton Road,
Horsham, West Sussex, RH13 5BB
© Maverick Arts Publishing Limited May 2023
+44 (0)1403 256941

A CIP catalogue record for this book is available at the British Library.

ISBN 978-1-84886-963-9

www.maverickbooks.co.uk

This book is rated as: White Band (Guided Reading)

Happily
Ever Arthur

By Jenny Jinks

Illustrated by
Michelle Simpson

Chapter 1

It was an ordinary, boring day and Arthur was on his way to school. On his way, he pretended to fight off a terrifying dragon, just like the hero in his favourite fairy tale.

Suddenly, Arthur thought he saw a snake on the path ahead. It was just a fallen branch, but Arthur didn't know that.

"Aaah!" screamed Arthur. He tripped and fell into a bush.

"Ouch!" Arthur said, hitting his head against something hard. There was a wishing well hidden in the middle of the bush.

What was that doing there?

Arthur dug in his pocket, pulled out a coin and made the same wish he always wished.

"I wish my life was more like a fairy tale," he said.

As Arthur threw the coin into the well, he began to feel dizzy. He leant against the well and closed his eyes.

When he opened them again, it was dark. Had he fallen asleep?

He tried to stand up, but there was something above him. He seemed to be in a long dark tunnel. Where was he?

The tunnel was just big enough to crawl down. Arthur crept along it, hoping he would find a way out.

Just as Arthur was beginning to think that the tunnel might never end, he came out into a gloomy little room. There were bars across one wall. It looked like a prison cell!

A loud roar came from somewhere above him. Arthur jumped.

"Where am I?" Arthur asked.

"The dungeons," croaked a creepy voice. And from out of the shadows stepped a witch!

Chapter 2

Arthur gasped. He had read a lot about wicked witches. He knew they were not to be trusted.

"Don't be frightened, I'll look after you. How did you get here?" the witch asked. "You've got a bump on your head. Let me help."

The witch took a step closer to Arthur and rummaged around in her cloak.

"No!" Arthur said a bit too loudly, taking a step

back. "I'm fine. Thanks."

"Suit yourself," the witch shrugged. Arthur was surprised to see her put a plaster back in her pocket.

The loud roar came again, shaking the dungeon walls.

"What is that?" Arthur asked.

"That, my dear," the witch said, "is my poor dragon."

"Dragon?" Arthur gasped.

"Yes. That evil princess captured him and locked him up in the tower," the witch said sadly.

Arthur couldn't believe it. A wicked witch that might not be so wicked? And an evil princess that captured dragons? It was like Arthur had walked into a weird fairy tale.

Arthur looked around at the creepy dungeon.

"I need to get out of here," he said. He looked for the tunnel but it seemed to have vanished.

"Don't worry. Once we get to my dragon, he'll get us out of here," the witch said.

"So how do we get to your dragon?" Arthur asked excitedly.

"That's where I'm stuck," the witch said, scratching her head. "I was hoping you might be able to help."

"Me?!" said Arthur. "How can I help?"

Before the witch could answer, they heard footsteps on the stairs.

"Quick, hide!" the witch told Arthur.

Arthur pushed himself against the wall and the tunnel magically appeared again. He tucked himself inside.

A beautiful princess appeared. She didn't look evil at all.

"Are you ready to talk?" she asked sweetly.

The witch didn't answer.

The dust in the dungeon made Arthur's nose itch. He needed to sneeze. He tried to stop it but...

Chapter 3

"ACHOOOOO!"

"What was that?"
the princess snapped,
looking around.

Arthur stayed as still as a statue.

The princess glared at the witch. "Looks like
you'll have to stay down here a little longer!"
the princess cried, and she stormed off.

"What does she want from you?" Arthur asked once the princess had gone.

"Magic," said the witch. "Dragon scales are magic, you see. Just a few dragon scales would give her more power than she ever dreamed of. No one would be safe!"

"But she's already got your dragon, hasn't she?" Arthur said.

"Yes, but she can't get near him without getting scorched," the witch smiled. "I'm the only one who knows how, and I'll never tell her!"

"So how *do* you get near a dragon?" Arthur asked.

The witch looked Arthur up and down thoughtfully.

"I can't tell you that... How do I know I can trust you?" she said.

"Trust me?" laughed Arthur.

"You might steal my dragon for yourself," the witch said.

"I would never do that," Arthur said. "I promise."

The witch didn't look sure.

"So, if we can get to your dragon, he could get us out of here?" Arthur asked.

"Oh yes, easily," the witch replied. "The only

problem is he's tied up in the tallest tower and we're locked up down here. And, even if we weren't locked up, we'd still have to get past the princess."

Arthur was thinking quickly. He had an idea. "I think I can get us to your dragon."

Arthur quickly whispered his idea to the witch. Now all they had to do was wait.

Chapter 4

A little while later, the princess came down to check on her prisoner again. But when she looked inside, the prison cell was empty.

"She's escaped!" the princess cried. She opened up the cell and searched inside.

"NOW!" shouted Arthur.

Arthur and the witch rushed out of the tunnel. As Arthur had hoped, it had appeared again when they needed it.

They ran past the princess, out through the open cell door, and slammed it shut behind them. The princess was locked inside.

They raced up the steps, out of the dungeon,
and off to find the dragon. The princess
screamed angrily as they went.

Finally, they reached the very top of the tallest
tower. They could hear the huge dragon on the
other side of the door.

Arthur couldn't help feeling a little scared. He had read enough about dragons to know how fierce they could be, but he was starting to realise he couldn't trust everything he read in fairy tales.

"So, we just walk in there, jump on his back and ride out of here?" Arthur asked nervously.

"Yes. As long as you've got this," the witch smiled, passing him some broccoli.

"Broccoli?" Arthur laughed. "*That's* the secret to taming a dragon?"

"Oh yes, they go mad for it. Give him a bit of broccoli and he's as tame as a tabby cat. Try it."

She gave Arthur a gentle push towards the door.

"Go on, he won't hurt you!"

Chapter 5

Arthur was a little worried this might be a trap. But he trusted his new friend.

He took a deep breath and, with the broccoli clutched tightly in his fist, he pushed the door open.

Arthur and the dragon stood face to face. The dragon growled. His fiery breath blazed past Arthur's cheeks.

Arthur held the broccoli out and waited.
The dragon stopped growling and sniffed.
He sniffed again.

Then he rolled over on the floor and made a
funny sound. Arthur laughed. Was he purring?

The witch gave the dragon some broccoli to eat,
and he chewed happily while they untied the
ropes around his wings and legs.

"Let's go home," the witch said.

"Home?" Arthur said. "I don't know how to get home."

"Don't worry, I'll make sure you get back safely. Now hop on!"

They climbed onto the dragon's back. Arthur expected them to head out of the door, but the witch turned the dragon around to face the tower wall.

"Hold on tight," the witch said.

The dragon charged straight at the brick wall.

Arthur closed his eyes and hugged the dragon's neck.

CRASH! The dragon smashed through the wall and flew off into the sky.

Arthur opened his eyes. They were flying way up high over hills and rivers. Arthur decided that flying on a dragon was his favourite thing in the world.

Chapter 6

Finally, the dragon came down to land and they climbed off.

"What will happen to the princess?" Arthur asked. "Will you let her go?"

"Of course, dear. I'm not wicked! Hopefully she has learnt her lesson," the witch smiled. "You know, the kingdom could use a brave hero like you."

"Brave? Hero?" Arthur laughed. "That's not me."

"Of course it is. You rescued me and my dragon," the witch said.

"Well thanks, but I should get back. My parents will be worried."

"In that case, you'd better take this," the witch said, handing him something small and shiny — a dragon scale!

"Just tell it where you want to go," the witch said. "And who knows, maybe we'll see each other again someday." She leant forward and gave Arthur a hug.

Arthur held the dragon scale in his hand and thought about home.

Suddenly, he began to feel very sleepy.

When Arthur opened his eyes, it was dark. He was on the floor, leaning against the wishing well. He was home.

Arthur sighed as he clambered out of the bush. He couldn't believe his fairy tale adventure was over.

Then he felt something in his pocket. He reached in and pulled out something shiny. A dragon scale!

Maybe this wasn't the end after all.
Maybe his adventures were just beginning!

The End

Book Bands for Guided Reading

The Institute of Education book banding system is a scale of colours that reflects the various levels of reading difficulty. The bands are assigned by taking into account the content, the language style, the layout and phonics. Word, phrase and sentence level work is also taken into consideration.

Maverick Early Readers are a bright, attractive range of books covering the pink to white bands. All of these books have been book banded for guided reading to the industry standard and edited by a leading educational consultant.

To view the whole Maverick Readers scheme, visit our website at www.maverickearlyreaders.com

Or scan the QR code above to view our scheme instantly!

Pink
Red
Yellow
Blue
Green
Orange
Turquoise
Purple
Gold
White